May 2021

Seth,

It was such a joy
to be your teacher
this year. I hope you
have a wonderful
summer. Love you!

Miss Hecker

WHEN YOU WANT SOMETHING TOO MUCH

Gus Loses His Grip

DAVID POWLISON

Editor

JOE HOX

Illustrator

Story creation by Jocelyn Flenders, a homeschooling mother, writer, and editor living in suburban Philadelphia. A graduate of Lancaster Bible College with a background in intercultural studies and counseling, the Good News for Little Hearts series is her first published work for children.

New Growth Press, Greensboro, NC 27404
Text copyright © 2019 by David Powlison
Illustration copyright © 2019 by New Growth Press

Cover/Interior Design and Typesetting: Trish Mahoney, themahoney.com

ISBN: 978-1-948130-77-6

LCCN 2019945102

Printed in India

28 27 26 25 24 23 22 21   3 4 5 6 7

"Taste and see that
the LORD is good.
Oh, the joys of those
who take refuge in him!"

Psalm 34:8

Mulberry Meadow was
lined with towering trees.

In the hollow of the Great Maple lived
Papa, Mama, Gus, and Gwen Raccoon.

One evening, as they ventured across
the pond for a bite to eat, Gus hopped
on a log and dashed to the other side.
He wanted to be the first to get to
the strawberry patch on the other
side of the pond.

As he quickly filled his paws with strawberries, Mama joked,
"Gus, be sure to save some for the rest of us!"

Gus loved berries: strawberries, raspberries, blackberries—any berries!
He also loved sugar snap peas and sweets from the candy shop.

Gus loved sweets.
He loved everything sweet!

Gwen exclaimed, "These strawberries are great. And tomorrow is Easter. We'll get lots of goodies!" Gus paused to picture his basket filled with luscious sweets.

Later that evening, Gus climbed into bed and peeked under his pillow—where he kept his secret stash of sweets.

He knew the rules—no candy in his bedroom! But Gus needed sweets, especially before bed.

He reached under his pillow.
Now where could they be?

He searched inside the pillowcase.
He threw back the covers and searched some more.
He paced the floor.

Where did his candy go?!

And then he remembered—he ate it all last night.
Every last piece.

He simply couldn't stop. And now he had nothing.
I'll never fall asleep, he thought. He collapsed on the bed and
stared at the ceiling. Finally he did fall asleep.

The next morning, Gus rubbed his tired eyes. He felt dreadful— until he remembered it was Easter.

He raced down the stairs to find his basket stuffed with green grass and mounds of sweets—

maple-covered eggs, gummy worms, and fruit leathers! His eyes grew wide as he dug his paws deep into his basket.

Mama said,
"Good morning, Gus!
Remember: no sweets
till after breakfast.

Papa's ready to read the
Easter story from the
Great Book. Let's gather
around the table."

As was their tradition, the Raccoon family listened to Papa read from the Great
Book the wonderful story of how God sent his own Son, Jesus, to love his people
and die for their sins. When Papa got to the best part—"The tomb is empty!
Jesus rose from the dead!"—Gus wasn't really listening. He kept thinking
about his sweets. He completely missed the sweetness of the story.

As soon as Papa closed the Great Book
and they finished breakfast,
Gus rushed to his basket.

He devoured an egg.
He crammed three gummy worms
into his mouth.

Then he reached for a fruit leather
and Papa said,
"All right, Gus. That's enough.
It's time to get ready for church."

Several days later, Gus's basket was empty but he was still craving more sweets. Mama was writing her shopping list and gathering bags for the market.

She called, "Gus! Gwen! Time to go!" The kits raced down the stairs. Papa said, "I'll meet you there! Gus can help me fish for dinner."

Once they arrived at the market, Mama zipped from stand to stand, with Gwen and Gus in tow. She was happily purchasing food and fabric and fancy trinkets. Raccoons love a bargain! At each new shop, she seemed to find another thing she needed to have, and the after-Easter prices were great!

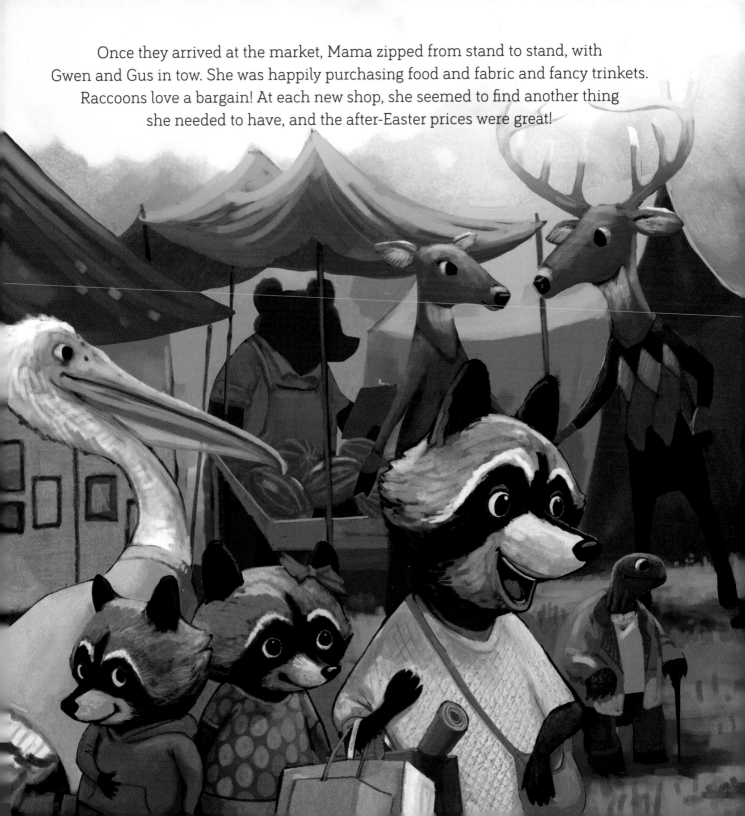

Even Mr. Hogster's candy shop was having a sale!

Gus exclaimed, "I'd like some candy!"
Mama replied, "You have plenty of candy at home."

Mama didn't know that Gus had
already eaten all of his Easter candy.
And Gus didn't tell her.

Mr. Hogster called,
"You're welcome to try a piece if it's
okay with your mom. Look, your
friend Lyle is at the counter right
now, choosing his piece."

As the moms chatted together and Mr. Hogster helped another customer, they didn't notice what was happening behind them at the candy counter. Lyle was taking more and more samples—filling his cheeks, paws, and pockets to the brim! He winked at Gus, who also began filling his paws.

Moments later, Papa arrived and upon seeing all of Mama's bags, exclaimed, "Goodness, Mama! We'll have bags hanging from our tails! Where are we going to put all of this stuff?"

Mama replied,
"Just a couple more stands to go!"

Gwen happily trailed behind Mama.
Papa held out his paw to Gus and said,
"I'm sure the fish are biting! Let's go."

Hogster's Sweets

Papa reached for Gus's paw and found it full of sweets!

All of a sudden,
Gus lost his grip!

The candy in his paws dribbled to the ground, like
a leaking faucet—
as if in slow motion, one piece after another.

Candy eggs, leathers, gummies, and berries
covered the ground, and Gus looked sadly down.

He thought,
Now I'm in trouble!
And he was.

Papa's eyes widened. "How did you get all this candy?"

Gus whispered,
"Mr. Hogster's store. He told Lyle and me
to take one, but then we couldn't stop."

Papa said, "We're going to return
all this to Mr. Hogster right now."

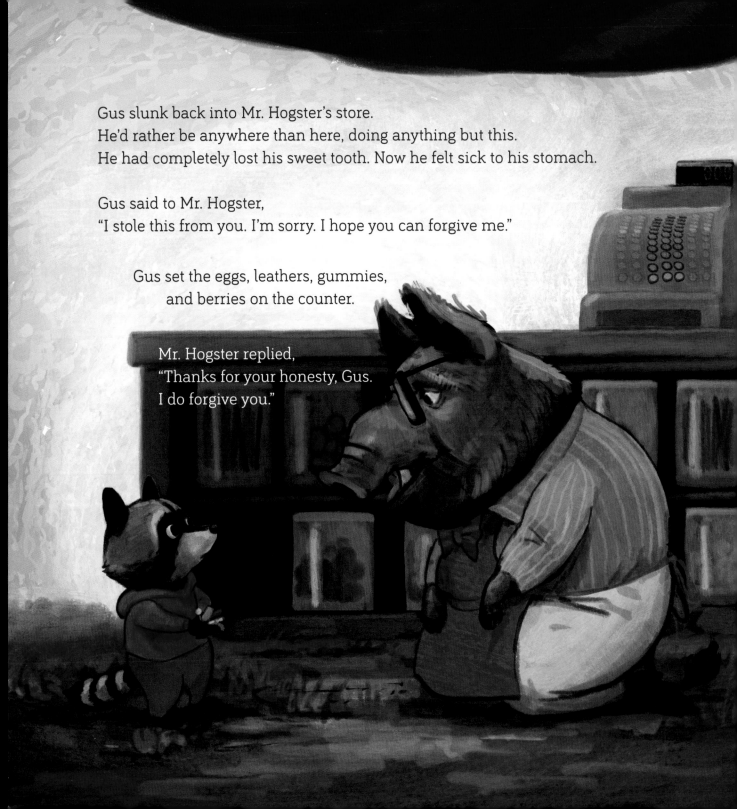

Gus slunk back into Mr. Hogster's store.
He'd rather be anywhere than here, doing anything but this.
He had completely lost his sweet tooth. Now he felt sick to his stomach.

Gus said to Mr. Hogster,
"I stole this from you. I'm sorry. I hope you can forgive me."

Gus set the eggs, leathers, gummies,
and berries on the counter.

Mr. Hogster replied,
"Thanks for your honesty, Gus.
I do forgive you."

As Papa and Gus walked away, Papa noticed a sale sign above Hedgehog's Hardware Store: 50% Off Fishing Lures.

Papa said, "Let's stop in. I just need a couple more lures."

After several minutes, Papa filled an entire shopping basket and was eyeing the fly rods. Gus tugged on Papa's paw and Papa said, "Okay, let's go. I'll come back later."

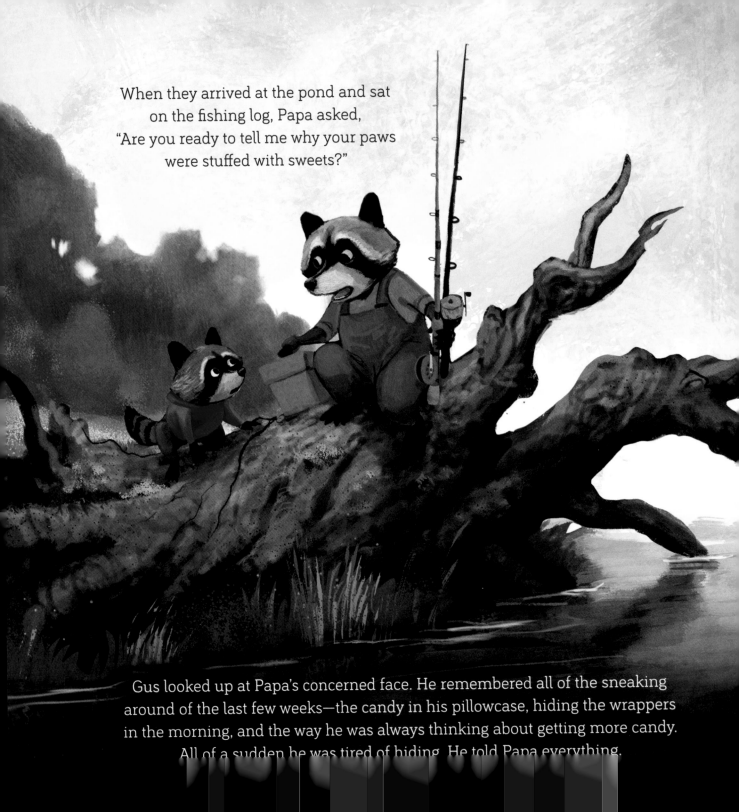

When they arrived at the pond and sat
on the fishing log, Papa asked,
"Are you ready to tell me why your paws
were stuffed with sweets?"

Gus looked up at Papa's concerned face. He remembered all of the sneaking
around of the last few weeks—the candy in his pillowcase, hiding the wrappers
in the morning, and the way he was always thinking about getting more candy.
All of a sudden he was tired of hiding. He told Papa everything.

Papa asked, "Did eating all that candy make you happy?"

"When I was eating it, I felt great, but then I always wanted more.
And I keep thinking about how to get more and more.

Now, I feel awful," Gus replied.

Papa looked at his own bag from Hedgehog's Hardware. He looked
at his new fishing pole. Then he said, "You're not the only one who
wants more and more. I think I can learn a lesson too."

Papa continued, "You know, Gus, there's nothing wrong with eating candy every once in awhile. You know God made sweets for us to enjoy. I think Jesus must have liked sweets too! But when we love something too much it gets a grip on us and we lose our grip on what is really important. We want something more than we love Jesus; we lose our grip on what makes us really happy. The Great Book calls that sin.

Gus said, "It reminds me of when I thought I needed my Easter basket more than hearing the story of how Jesus saves me from what I do wrong."

Papa agreed. "Yes! You're not alone, Gus. Mama and I struggle too. I'm beginning to see all the areas where God might want me to lose my grip! You know that's why we need Jesus. We can't stop eating too many sweets, buying too many trinkets at the market, or buying too many fishing lures and poles without help from him. What we think we need grips us, but our sin is not too strong for Jesus!"

Papa took a pencil and two scraps of paper from the pocket of his overalls. "Here is a verse from the Great Book that we all need to remember," he said.

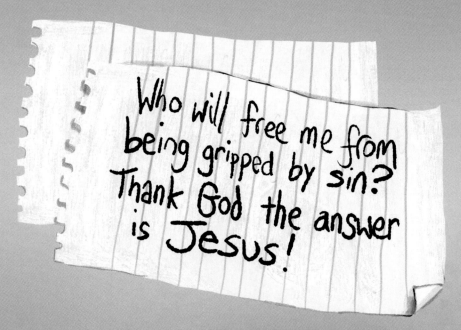

Who will free me from being gripped by sin? Thank God the answer is Jesus!

He wrote it twice and handed one to Gus and tucked one into his overall pocket.

Gus laughed and said, "Now we can remind each other that only Jesus can help us lose our grip."

"Yes," said Papa, "when Jesus holds us we learn to loosen our grip on the things we hold too tightly."

And once we lose our grip on what we want, we can
notice all the wonderful, sweet things God has given us to enjoy.
The Great Book says, 'Taste and see that the LORD is good.'
Look around at all the things you can see that the Lord has given us."

"Well," said Gus slowly,
"I can see and
hear a red bird singing.
That's pretty sweet.

I can feel a breeze blowing,
and that's pretty sweet on a hot day.

And having time to fish
with you makes me really happy!"

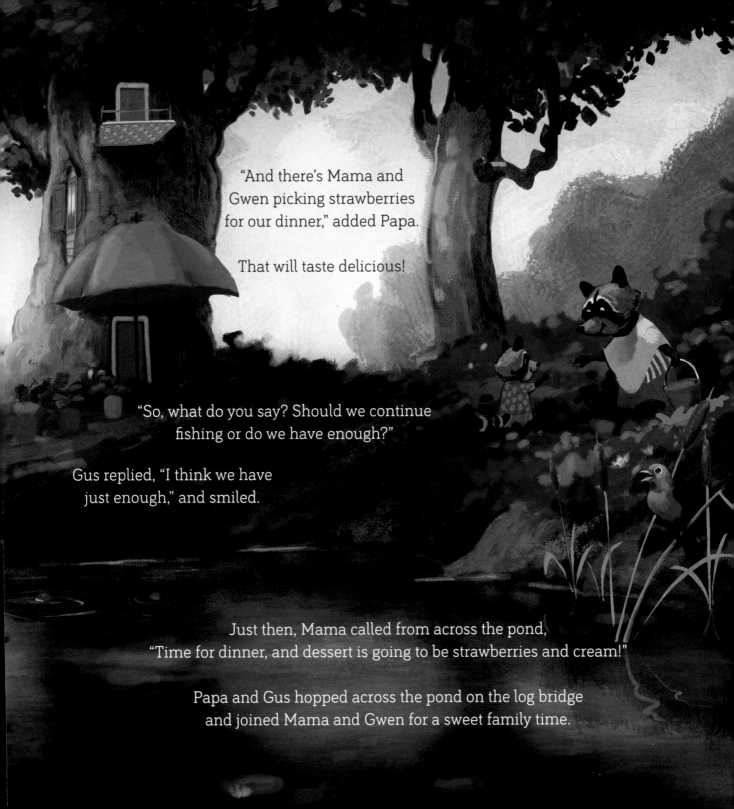

"And there's Mama and Gwen picking strawberries for our dinner," added Papa.

That will taste delicious!

"So, what do you say? Should we continue fishing or do we have enough?"

Gus replied, "I think we have just enough," and smiled.

Just then, Mama called from across the pond,
"Time for dinner, and dessert is going to be strawberries and cream!"

Papa and Gus hopped across the pond on the log bridge
and joined Mama and Gwen for a sweet family time.

Helping Your Child with the "I Wantsies"

As Gus found out, it's easy to go from "I'd like to have" to "I must have." In our family we called this the "I wantsies." Often the "I wantsies" start with wanting a good thing—something sweet to eat (nothing wrong with that!), the love of someone special, a friendship, or even good health. But when we want even a good thing too much, then, as Gus found out, it takes charge of us. Of course, Gus wasn't the only one in this story who wanted a good thing too much—Papa liked to collect lots of fishing equipment and Mama liked getting more and more stuff for the house. So helping your children with the "I wantsies" starts by acknowledging that you need help as much as they do. You can learn together about the grace and mercy of Jesus for people who want good things too much, as well as for people who want bad things. Gus started out wanting a good thing—a sweet taste—and ended up wanting bad things—lying and stealing. Here are some truths for you and your children to remember when you are gripped by the "I wantsies."

1 **Gus's desire for candy eventually took charge of what he thought and did.** What started as a temptation (wanting more and more sweets), led Gus to eat too much candy, lie, and eventually steal. James says "Temptation comes from our own desires, which entice us and drag us away. These desires give birth to sinful actions. And when sin is allowed to grow, it gives birth to death" (James 1:14–15). Here's a rule of thumb: sins start out small, but they always grow bigger.

2 **Our desires are powerful.** Gus was not able to stop himself from eating all his candy. His own will power was not powerful enough. What is powerful enough to set us free from wanting a good thing too much or from wanting a bad thing? The Apostle Paul points us to Jesus, "Who will free me from this life that is dominated by sin and death? Thank God! The answer is in Jesus Christ our Lord" (Romans 7:24-25). The truth is that we can't free ourselves from desires that have mastered us. Only Jesus can. Papa points this out to Gus and paraphrases this verse for Gus, so Gus can connect it to his struggle.

3 **How does Jesus free us?** Remind your child of the sweet Easter story—Jesus died and rose from the dead, so that all who believe in him will be forgiven and given a new life. The same power that raised Jesus from the dead is now ours when we trust in Jesus. Peter says, "God's power has given us everything we need to lead a godly life. All of this has come to us because we know the God who chose us. He chose us because of his own glory and goodness. He has also given us his very great and valuable promises. He did it so you could share in his nature. You can share in it because

you've escaped from the evil in the world. This evil is caused by sinful desires" (2 Peter 1:3–4). Because of Jesus's death we can be forgiven and because of his resurrection, we can be filled with God's strength that changes even our deepest desires and makes us love what Jesus loves.

4 **Living for what you want separates us from God and people.** Gus hid his addiction to candy and how much he was eating from the people that loved him the most—his parents. He couldn't be honest with them or God. *But God gives us a way back to him*—we can always turn and say "sorry" to him and to others. That's what the Bible calls *repentance*. And repentance restores our relationship with God and with others. John says this "Suppose we claim we are without sin. Then we are fooling ourselves. The truth is not in us. But God is faithful and fair. If we confess our sins, he will forgive our sins. He will forgive every wrong thing we have done. He will make us pure (1 John 1:8–9 NIVR).

5 **Keep on asking God for the gift of his Spirit.** Turning from your own way doesn't happen just once. You turn to God every day. Jesus tells us to keep asking and seeking the help that we need from him (Luke 11:9–10). How does that help come to us? He goes on to say that our heavenly Father's best gift to his children is his Spirit (Luke 11:13). As we turn to Jesus and ask for forgiveness and his Spirit, he fills us with the same power that raised Jesus from the dead. That's the most powerful force in the universe. That is the power that can change our hearts, minds, and actions. That power can help Gus keep candy in the right place in his heart and can help Papa control his desire for fishing equipment. It can also change you and your child's struggle with the "I wantsies."

6 **True pleasure comes from enjoying God and his good gifts.** After Gus said, "Sorry," he was able to enjoy all the good things that God had put in his life—a bird singing, a cool breeze, hanging out with Papa fishing, and watching Mama and Gwen pick strawberries. There is a whole world of pleasure waiting for us on the other side of going to God and saying sorry for how we turn from him and go our own way. When the power of God comes into our lives, we lose our grip on our own desires, and we can "taste and see that the Lord is good" (Psalm 34:8). We take joy in knowing God, remembering that his mercies are new every morning and that his is always faithful (Lamentation 3:22–23). As our joy in knowing God grows so does our joy in all of the good things he has given us.

Back Pocket Bible Verses

Who will free me from this life
that is dominated by sin and death?
Thank God! The answer is in
Jesus Christ our Lord.

Romans 7:24-25

God's power has given us everything we need
to lead a godly life. All of this has come to
us because we know the God who chose us.
He chose us because of his own glory and
goodness. He has also given us his very great
and valuable promises. He did it so you could
share in his nature. You can share in it because
you've escaped from the evil in the world. This
evil is caused by sinful desires.

2 Peter 1:3-4 (NIRV)

Suppose we claim we are without sin.
Then we are fooling ourselves.
The truth is not in us. But God is
faithful and fair. If we confess our
sins, he will forgive our sins. He will
forgive every wrong thing we have
done. He will make us pure.

1 John 1:8-9 (NIRV)

"And so I tell you, keep on asking,
and you will receive what you ask
for. Keep on seeking, and you will
find. Keep on knocking, and the door
will be opened to you. For everyone
who asks, receives. Everyone who
seeks, finds. And to everyone who
knocks, the door will be opened."

Luke 11:9-10

Back Pocket Bible Verses

WHEN YOU WANT SOMETHING TOO MUCH

GOOD NEWS FOR LITTLE HEARTS

WHEN YOU WANT SOMETHING TOO MUCH

GOOD NEWS FOR LITTLE HEARTS

WHEN YOU WANT SOMETHING TOO MUCH

GOOD NEWS FOR LITTLE HEARTS

WHEN YOU WANT SOMETHING TOO MUCH

GOOD NEWS FOR LITTLE HEARTS